Mr Gum

and the
Biscuit Billionaire

Andy Stanton
Illustrated by David Tazzyman

EGMONT

Shabba me whiskers! Andy Stanton's *Mr Gum* is winner of the Roald Dahl Funny Prize, the Red House Children's Book Award AND the Blue Peter Book Award for The Most Fun Story With Pictures. AND he's been shortlisted for LOADS of other prizes too! It's barking bonkers!

PRAISE FOR *Mr Gum*:

'Do not even think about buying another book – This is gut-spillingly funty.' Alex, aged 13

'It's hilarious, it's brilliant . . . Stanton's the Guv'nor, The Boss.' Danny Baker, BBC London Radio

'Funniest book I have ever and will ever read . . . When I read this to my mum she burst out laughing and nearly wet herself . . . When I had finished the book I wanted to read it all over again it was so good.' Bryony, aged 8

'Funny? You bet.' Guardian

'Andy Stanton accumulates silliness and jokes in an irresistible, laughter-inducing romp.' Sunday Times

'Raucous, revoltingly rambunctious and nose-snortingly funny.' Daily Mail

'David Tazzyman's illustrations match the irreverent sparks of word wizardry with slapdash delight.' Junior Education

'This is weird, wacky and one in a million.' Primary Times

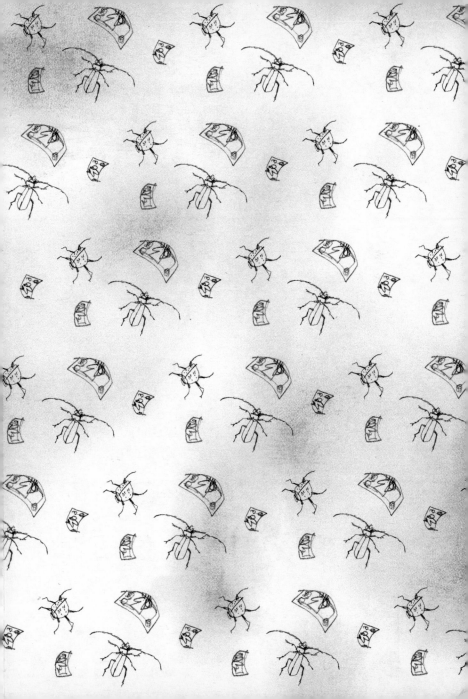

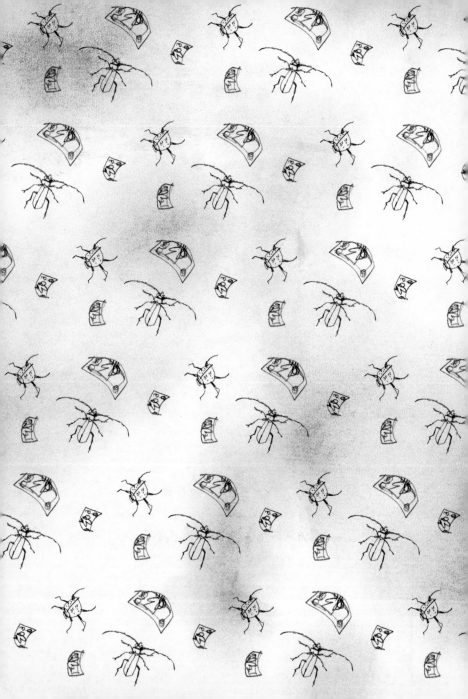

This one's for me brother, his name is Dan
And he looks like a marshy to the native man!

Mr Gum and the Biscuit Billionaire
First published 2007 by Egmont UK Limited
The Yellow Building, 1 Nicholas Road
London W11 4AN

Text copyright © 2007 Andy Stanton
Illustration copyright © 2007 David Tazzyman

The moral rights of the author and illustrator have been asserted

ISBN 978 0 6035 7361 3

mrgum.co.uk
www.jellypiecentral.co.uk
www.egmont.co.uk

A CIP catalogue record for this title is available from the British Library
Printed and bound in Great Britain by the CPI Group

67763/1

and the
Biscuit Billionaire

Andy Stanton

Illustrated by David Tazzyman

Contents

Chapter 1

On Boaster's Hill

It all started late one afternoon in the peaceful little town of Lamonic Bibber. Summer was almost at an end and the day stretched out long and lazy like a huge glossy panther made of time. The birds chirped in the trees, the rabbits chirped in their burrows, and a fox walked along the railway tracks whistling 'Greensleeves' and thinking fondly of a vixen he had once loved.

Up on Boaster's Hill a little girl sat reading a book called '**Cobbler Wins The Prizes**'. Now this little girl's name was Polly and she was the sort of girl you could be friends with. She was brilliant at running and jumping and scabbing up her knees and she didn't have no time for nonsense, OK? She was brave and honest and true and when she laughed the sunlight went splashing off her pretty teeth like diamonds in search of adventure.

But where were the laughter and diamondy teeth now? Nowhere, because Polly was bored.

"**Cobbler Wins The Prizes**' is full of escapades but that's just a book,' she complained to herself. 'Nothin' exciting never happens 'round here. An' that whopper dog Jake never even comes 'round to play no more!'

For alas, it was true. Polly hadn't seen big

Jake all summer long. Oh, how she missed riding on his huge furry back and pretending he was a horse or a spaceship!

 'Jakey!' she called hopefully, in case he just happened to be nearby, playing cards with a dormouse or something – but there was no answering woof to be heard.

'Sigh,' sighed Polly with a sigh. 'First no adventures an' now no Jakey. It's well unfair.'

And with that she lay back in the long grass. The hot sun beat down and soon she was drifting, drifting away . . .

When Polly awoke it was dusk and the afternoon had grown fat with shadows. A low breeze whispered secrets in the bushes and the light was all funny and golden, full of magic and mystery and moths.

'What strangery is this?' whispered Polly. Her hair was standing on end and her arms were covered in goosebumps. It felt like something was going to happen.

And then, sure enough, something did happen. A little figure appeared over the top of Boaster's Hill. It was the strangest little man Polly had ever pointed her eyes at. For a start, he was only 15.24 centimetres tall. And he was made entirely out of gingerbread, with raisins for eyes. And he had electric muscles so he could walk around like you or me, and blue sparks came off him whenever he moved. And what's more, he carried an enormous biscuit tin and it was stuffed full of money. And as you know, money is worth a lot of money. And there was an awful lot of money in that tin, and that's a fact.

'Hello,' said the little weirdy, skipping over to where Polly sat. 'I am Alan Taylor.'

'I'm Polly,' replied Polly in wonder. 'Are you from Fairymagic Dream Land where the rivers run with lemonade and the streets are paved with unicorns?'

'Please don't make fun of me,' said Alan Taylor. 'Haven't you ever seen a gingerbread man with electric muscles before?'

'Sorry, I haven't,' replied Polly in embarrassment. 'I'm only nine. And I didn't mean to make no fun.'

'Well, all right,' replied the talkative biscuit.
'Here, take some money so we can be friends!' he
continued, offering her a bundle of banknotes.

'Why, I don't need your riches,' said Polly
in astonishment, 'I'll be your friend anyway.'

'That's not how the world works,' said Alan
Taylor sadly, stuffing the money back into the
tin. 'But do come to my party tomorrow,' he said,
cheering up. 'I've just moved into town and built
a MASSIVE mansion on top of this very hill.

Look! It's MASSIVE so I can impress people and
get friends. It's MASSIVE.'

Polly looked up and there it stood, a-gleamin'
and a-glitterin' in a blaze of floodlights.

'Rimloff!' she exclaimed. 'It's big enough for
a king! Or two little kings. They could share it
and play hide-an'-seek.'

'But it's all mine!' laughed Alan Taylor. 'I am
so rich! I am so rich!' he sang, dancing around

in the grass and throwing banknotes at a passing aphid. 'Do you like me, Polly? Do you want some money?'

'I just told you,' said Polly firmly. 'That's not what *friendship* is all about.'

'Of course it is,' replied Alan Taylor with a frown. 'But listen. Come round tomorrow afternoon, before the party starts. I'll show you my house and impress you THAT way instead.'

Well, the truth was, Polly did want to see inside that marvellous house. And she liked Alan

Taylor, even though he seemed a bit confused about money and *friendship*. So she thanked him graciously. Then she tried to curtsey but she didn't know how, so she just wiggled her arms around and shouted 'CURTSEY!' and hoped that would do.

'Good try,' said Alan Taylor generously. 'Well, I'd better get going. There's lots more people to invite and impress!'

And off he raced on his crunchy little legs,

leaving Polly too excited for words. So she said some numbers instead.

'12! 93! 114!' she said as she made her way back home, and soon she was in bed, dreaming of gingerbread men and parties and all manner of wonderful things.

Chapter 2
Meanwhile, Over at Mr Gum's

Mr Gum was standing in front of the cracked mirror in the lonely bedroom of his grimsters old house. Blow me down with an oil tanker, he was a horror. He hated children, animals, fun and every cartoon ever made. What he liked was snoozing in bed all day. In fact, although it was eight o'clock in the evening Mr Gum had only just got up. For not only was he a horror, he was a lazer too.

So anyway. There he was in front of the mirror, getting ready to go out.

'You're up early, you handsome devil,' he said to his reflection. 'What do you fancy doin' today?'

'I fancies bein' even more evil than usual,' replied his reflection with a nasty laugh.

'Good idea, stupid,' said Mr Gum. 'In that case, I better look me most frightful.'

He got a felt-tip pen and drew some extra scowls on his forehead.

Then he scruffed up his big red beard to make it as wild and frightening as possible. It wasn't quite

16

terrifying enough so he stuck a couple of beetles in it and a photo of a shark.

'That should do it,' he growled. Then he sproinged downstairs, jumped on a skateboard he'd nicked off a six-year-old and headed into town.

On the high street, Martin Launderette was about to close up his launderette for the night when in came one last customer. It was Jonathan Ripples, the fattest man in town.

'Martin, please be careful with these,' he said, handing over a bundle of clothes. 'They're very delicate.'

'No problem, Big J,' said Martin Launderette reassuringly. 'I'll do them in cold water so they don't shrink or anything.'

But as he was putting the clothes into the machine he noticed someone skateboarding badly along the high street, scowling as he went.

'Look,' said Martin Launderette, 'it's Mr Gum! And he's going into Billy William the Third's!'

'Oh, dear,' said Jonathan Ripples nervously. 'That can only mean trouble.'

While JR's head was turned, Martin Launderette secretly turned the washing machine up from COLD WASH to SUPER HOT

SHRINK WASH. Then he took out a red notebook and wrote:

That fatty Ripples thinks he's so clever
but I'll have the last laugh!
His clothes won't even fit ME after this!

Meanwhile Mr Gum had jumped off his skateboard. He smashed it to bits, pulled all the wheels off and left it lying on the pavement to show everyone he was the best.

'I win again,' he smirked. Then he opened the door and went into Billy William the Third's Right Royal Meats.

Now Billy William was the most revolting butcher in England, and that's official.

A big greasy trophy stood in his shop window
and here is what it said:

England's Most
Revolting Butcher Trophy
Awarded to Billy William
for the twentieth year running,
in fact just keep the trophy forever –
you always win, there's no point
having the competition,
you really are disgusting.

So hardly anyone in town shopped there, even though it was the only butcher's around. Most people went to the next town to buy their meat or became vegetarian or only ate birdseed. But Mr Gum felt right at home there. Sometimes he wished the whole world could be exactly like Billy's: filled with entrails and slimy cow lips and rubbery old turkey necks. But he knew it would never happen. It was just a beautiful dream.

'Mornin', me old suitcase,' said Billy William as Mr Gum wafted in. 'Want some entrails?' he added, slurping up a load of bad meat off the counter with his grotty old tongue.

'No time for that, Caterpillar Joe!' replied Mr Gum, which is what he sometimes called Billy when he was over-excited with evil.

'You're over-excited with evil, ain'tcha?' said Billy. 'I can always tell.'

'It's true,' said Mr Gum, jumping up on the counter and dancing around in a bucket of pig's brains. 'I fancies doin' some terrible bad deeds today an' no mistake!'

'I know what'd be funty,' said Billy William, scratching his chin with a long unwashed finger. (He always pronounced the word 'funny' in this way. Pronouncing words strangely was one of his hobbies, like collecting phlegm or trying to see up ladies' skirts.) 'We could break a skateboard,' he suggested.

'Nah, I already done that,' said Mr Gum impatiently.

'OK,' said Billy William. 'How about we stand out on the street an' step on butterflies?'

'It just ain't evil enough, Billy!' said Mr Gum, kicking a cow's eyeball across the shop in frustration. 'What we gonna do?'

Just then the door opened and in came Alan Taylor. He'd been all over town, inviting people to his party and giving out money (or 'making

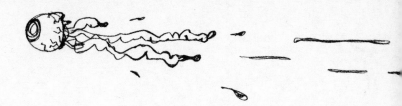

friends', as he called it). Unfortunately no one had warned him about Billy William's, otherwise he'd have kept well away. And as soon as he opened the door and slipped on an eyeball he knew he'd made a biffer of a mistake. But Alan Taylor was a gentleman born and bread, and he remembered his manners as best he could.

'Greetings!' he gabbled, bravely ignoring all the blood and guts and the pile of strange twisty bones in the corner. 'I am Alan Taylor and I'm

having a party tomorrow night on Boaster's
Hill! Do come along. You'd be most welco–'

A hairy old pig's head fell off a hook, slid
down the wall and came rolling slowly towards
him. With that, the last of Alan Taylor's
courage disappeared. He gave a little yelp,
threw a handful of money into the air and ran
back outside to safety.

'Did you see that?' said Mr Gum, stuffing
the cash down his pants where no one would

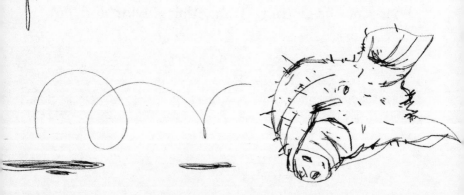

dare to go after it, not even Billy William.

'I did,' replied the dreadful butcher. 'That little tungler's as rich as a mushroom!'

'Now listen,' Mr Gum continued slyly, 'I wants that money, not just a bit of it but the whole burpin' lot. But we'll need a plan, an' that's where you come in, you enormous guff merchant. So get hatchin' plans like you never hatched plans before!'

'Righty-oh,' smirked Billy William, and with that he closed his eyes and began hatching a plan in perfect silence. He was like a horrible hen, except he hatched plans instead of eggs and the plans grew into misery instead of chickens, and he didn't have wings or a beak or feathers and he didn't make clucking noises and he wasn't a hen.

Four hours later Billy William opened his eyes.

'Right, I've got it,' he said. 'We'll go to Taylor's stupid party, then when it's dark we sneak up on him an' take his biscuit tin. Then we escape to France, change our names an' live like powerful kings on all the cash.'

'Caterpillar Joe, you're a genius!' laughed Mr Gum through a mouthful of entrails. 'A blibberin' genius!'

Chapter 3
Alan Taylor Shows Off Like Nobody's Fat Business

The following afternoon, Polly met her good friend Friday O'Leary at the bottom of Boaster's Hill and together they set off for Alan

Taylor's house. For some reason, Friday was coated from head to foot in pomegranate seeds. However, Polly knew better than to ask questions for Friday's ways were deep and mysterious.

It's just one of his 'credible wisdoms, I expects, thought Polly and she was right. For as they climbed the hill, the birds of the air swooped down and pecked away the seeds. By the time they reached the top, not a single one remained.

'The seeds will decorate their nests and

guard against cuckoos,' nodded Friday wisely as the last chaffinch flew off. ''Tis nature's way.'

But then he saw the huge white mansion sparkling in the sunshine and his eyes exploded in amazement.

'THE TRUTH IS A LEMON MERINGUE!' he shouted, as he sometimes liked to do. 'It's MASSIVE!'

At that, Alan Taylor ran out to greet them, his delicious face flushed with excitement.

'Polly!' he laughed, throwing money at her. 'And this must be your friend, Friday O'Leary!'

For you see, Friday was wearing a t-shirt which said:

**My name is Friday O'Leary.
I'm Polly's friend.**

'But where's my manners?' said their little host. 'You must be hungry after your long walk.'

He snapped his fingers and at once a servant scuttled out of the house holding a silver tray of sandwiches. Really really posh ones. But there was no time to eat them because Alan Taylor snapped his fingers again and a sports car appeared.

'Hop in!' shouted Alan Taylor and the next thing you know, the car zoomed into the mansion, yep, seriously – just right in through the front door. Round the rooms the car whizzed, smashing up Chinese vases and knocking over antique furniture.

FTOING! They ran over a grandfather clock, killing it instantly.

'Don't worry,' Alan Taylor laughed, 'I'm so rich I can easily afford another one!'

Why, thought Polly, *he's just like a little kid showing off. Why don't he just do proper trusts in people 'stead of tryin' to impress them?*

But the little biscuit was snapping his fingers once more.

'To the Alancopter!' he cried,

bundling Polly and Friday into a helicopter which stood in the dining room. He fired it up and out they flew, smashing straight through a stained glass window. Over the hillside they soared, faster and faster until Polly's head was spinning like a daffodil. Alan Taylor was an absolutely rubbish pilot, and he kept nearly hitting trees and peregrine falcons, so everyone (including himself) was secretly relieved when he brought the Alancopter back down, making a perfect landing in a fish pond. Out they all climbed, dizzy and exhausted.

'Please, sir,' began Polly weakly. 'Can I gets a glass of wate–'

But Alan Taylor was dancing around like a biscuit possessed.

'No time!' he cried. 'Look! The party's about to start!'

And turning around, Polly saw funfair rides, lots and lots of them dotted all over the hillside. And there were stripy tents and lights in the trees, and the smell of candyfloss it was in the air, so it was. And down below, waiting excitedly at the bottom of the hill, was a tremendous crowd. Nearly all the townsfolk had turned up. Jonathan Ripples was eating a tub of margarine and Martin Launderette was there too, writing in his red notebook. Beany McLeany, who loved things that rhymed, was doing a showbiz quiz on a girl named Liz. A little girl called Peter was there with her dad, whose name was Rachel. And there were

hundreds of others besides. Hundreds, I tell you.

Alan Taylor snapped his fingers and all at once the sky was ablaze with fireworks, soaring and fizzing overhead.

'Hooray for the Biscuit Billionaire!' roared the crowd and they ran up the hill to join the party.

🍷 🍷 🍷

Well, what larks. You should have been there! The jugglers juggled, the clowns clowned and the

toilet cleaners cleaned the toilets. Fire eaters ate fire, water drinkers drank water and a lion put its head in the mouth of a lion tamer. In one corner a fat man displayed his amazing belly for all to see, it wasn't part of the show, it was just Jonathan Ripples because his shirt had shrunk in the wash.

'Let's try the Ghost Train, Polly,' grinned Alan Taylor. 'There's real ghosts in there!'

'Yippee!' cried Polly. 'I wants to see a ghost ever so much!'

'**There be no such thing as ghosts!**' said Friday scornfully. '**It be all fool-talk, lock, stock, and barrel; that's what it be, an' nowt else. These bans an' wafts an' boh-ghosts an' barguests and bogles an' all anent them is only fit to set bairns an' dizzy women a-belderin'. They be nowt but air-blebs!**'

Alan Taylor and Polly stood staring at him, their mouths wide open.

'Um, Friday,' said Polly eventually. 'What you on about?'

'Dunno,' Friday shrugged, climbing on to the Ghost Train. 'But it sounded good.'

So after all that, Polly finally got to meet some ghosts and they were very friendly.

One of them gave her some new shoes, and Friday made friends with a tiny phantom called Pickles and got its email address.*

*picklestheghost@notveryalive.com

And after that, Polly went on the fastest rollercoaster in the world, so fast that you couldn't even remember if you'd been on it or not, your only proof was that you could hardly walk afterwards and you were covered in your own sick.

Meanwhile, Jonathan Ripples had eaten one burger too many and his stomach was groaning like a shipwreck.

'I think I'd better lie down,' he said unhappily.

He staggered out of the food tent, lay down on the hillside and closed his eyes. No sooner had he done so than Martin Launderette ran up and stuck a sign by his head which said: Ride the BOUNCY CASTLE!

'Look!' exclaimed a little kid excitedly. 'A new ride!' And within seconds there were tonnes of little kids jumping up and down on Jonathan Ripples, screaming and laughing as they played in the flab.

Martin Launderette was hiding in a nearby bush.

Ha, Ha, he wrote in his red notebook. My best trick yet - turning Ripples into a fairground attraction!

But Martin Launderette's trick was no way the worst thing that happened on Boaster's Hill that night. There was much worse stuff about to happen, believe you me.

Chapter 4
The Onions of Doom

On the other side of the hill, two shadowy figures were creeping along with shenanigans on their minds and entrails in their mouths. Of course, it was Mr Gum and Caterpillar Joe, sorry, I mean Billy William the Third. Halfway up the hill they stopped and lay down like soldiers, but not the ones on *your* side – the other lot.

Mr Gum scanned the party through some evil binoculars. 'Shabba me whiskers,' he grimaced. 'People having fun – I can't stands it! Hang on – there's Taylor!'

'Has he got that there biscuit tin wiv 'im?' asked Billy William, licking his dirty lips and burping at the same time just to see if it was possible.

'Yeah,' said Mr Gum, chuckling so hard an entrail shot out his nostril. 'An' soon it'll be ours.'

Back at the party Polly and Friday were climbing on to the Big Wheel.

'Have fun, you two,' said Alan Taylor. 'I'm off to get a hot dog.'

'Bring me one,' Friday called cheerily after him as the chair rose up into the night sky. 'And make sure it's got millions of onions!'

What a view greeted Friday and Polly when they reached the top of the wheel. All of Lamonic Bibber was spread out before them like a mighty pancake sprinkled with houses. To the west the mountains challenged the heavens with their height and to the east the sea challenged the heavens by being flat and wet and not really challenging the heavens after all.

'It's so beautiful,' sighed Polly as they sat there at the top of the world, the carriage creaking softly to and fro in the breeze. She gazed down and saw the party far below. The people looked like ants and the ants looked like even smaller ants. And further down the hillside Polly could see tonnes of little kids jumping up and down on some sort of bouncy castle.

I still wishes Jake was here though, she thought, shivering a little in the night air. *Everything's more fun when that fat old woofdog's around.*

☆ ☆ ☆

Meanwhile, Alan Taylor was yib-yabbin' along after some dogs of a different kind. Hot dogs. As he went, the townsfolk bent down to pat his back and cheer him on his way.

'It's the best party in the last one hundred years!' exclaimed Old Granny, the oldest woman in Lamonic Bibber. 'Alan Taylor, you are the champ!'

'You're a treasure! It's a pleasure to enjoy such leisure,' rhymed Beany McLeany.

'I admire you, Alan Taylor, for you are a noble and generous fellow,' said a six-month-old baby. And her mother rejoiced for these were the first words her infant daughter had ever spoken.

The praise rang in Alan Taylor's ears and the lights of the fair danced in his vision and he felt as if he were in a magical dream where he would always be safe from harm.

'Everyone's my friend now,' he said fiercely to himself. 'No one will ever laugh at me again like they did at school.'

At last he came to the hot dog stand which stood in the shadows on the very edge of the fairground. It was quieter here. The laughter and the music sounded far off in the distance and a cold wind had struck up, whistling softly through the trees as if to warn that shenanigans were afoot. But Alan Taylor suspected nothing.

'Two hot dogs, please,' he said. 'With millions of onions.'

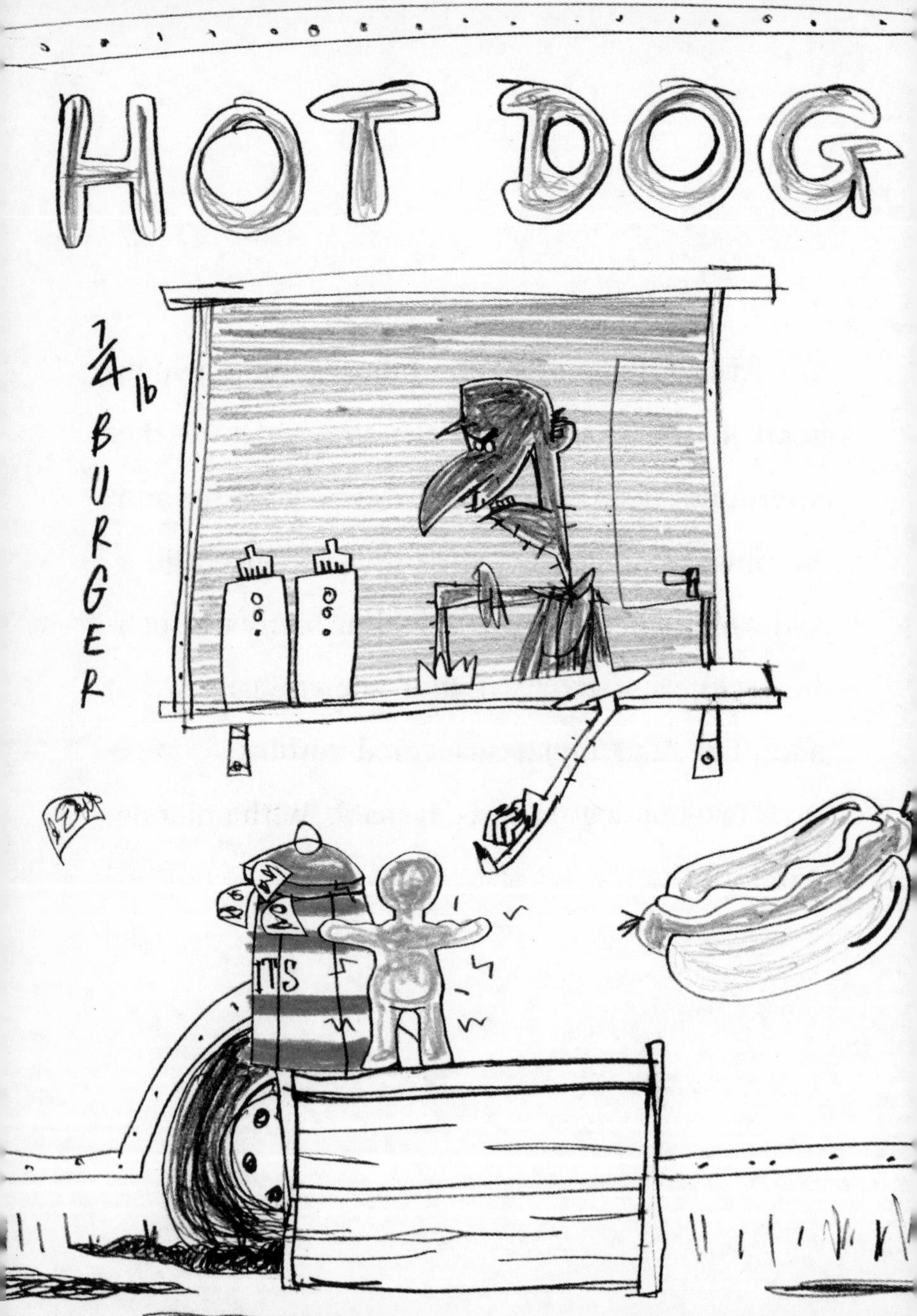
HOT DOG
1/4 lb
BURGER
ITS

'Onions, you says?' remarked the hot dog man, his face half-hidden in the shadows. His words stretched out long and low, slippery as rattlesnakes. 'I'll gives you onions all right!'

'OK, then,' said Alan Taylor innocently.

'Hop up here, me little ginger,' said the hot dog man, beckoning with a long unwashed finger. 'I likes to get a good look at me customers.'

So Alan Taylor hopped up on to the hot dog stand, a tiny shining beacon of trust in the cold starry night.

'Now, about those onions –' he began.

'Come closer, me little ginger,' murmured the hot dog man. 'Closer to the onions.'

Alan Taylor took a step towards the big pile of onions which crackled and sizzled on the grill.

'Another step, me little ginger,' whispered the hot dog man. 'Thaaat's right . . . Now one step more . . .'

And then, in a flash, someone jumped out from behind a leaf and grabbed the biscuit tin from Alan Taylor's grasp.

'Shenanigans!' squealed the Biscuit Billionaire but it was too late. The hot dog man had scooped him up and stuffed him into a bun.

'There you go!' shrieked the hot dog man, piling on handful after handful of onions and slapping the whole mess down on the counter. 'Have all the onions you want! No extra charge!'

And with a terrible laugh, the two robbers turned and ran off down the hill as fast as their bad legs could run.

'We done it!' howled Billy William, tearing off his disguise. Because I know this will surprise you but . . .

HE WAS THE HOT DOG MAN ALL ALONG!

'An' who's ever gonna know it was us what done the robbin's?' chortled Mr Gum, brandishing the biscuit tin as he ran. 'No one, that's who!'

But it wasn't 'no one, that's who!' It was 'Friday and Polly, that's who!' From up on the Big Wheel, they had seen every horrible moment. And as soon as they were back down, they wasted no time in legging it over to the hot dog stand like the heroes they were. They made it just in time to see Jonathan Ripples reaching for a hot dog smothered in onions.

He brought it to his flabulous lips.

He opened his food-destroying mouth.

He licked a bit of ketchup off the bun.

'POWERJUMP!' cried Polly, leaping headfirst at Jonathan Ripples' stomach, and down he went, the hot dog flying from his grasp and landing in Friday's hair. With a dizzy moan, Alan Taylor emerged from the bun, smothered in sauce and onions, slithered down Friday's nose and landed on the grass in a sloppy heap. Jonathan Ripples took one look at what he'd almost eaten and fainted away like a right wibber.

'Where's my biscuit tin?' spluttered Alan Taylor weakly. 'All my money was in there! Now I've got nothing!'

And even as he said these words, one of his servants pulled a switch and all the lights went out. The rides ground to a halt, the jugglers dropped their hoops and a clown turned into a businessman in a grey suit who never smiled and told lies all the time.

For Alan Taylor was no longer the Biscuit Billionaire. He was just the Biscuit and the fun was over.

Chapter 5
The Robbers on the Run

As midnight struck, the two robbers were racing away over the dark muddy fields in their hobnail boots, churning up great clods of earth in their wake and ruining the farmers' crops. The biscuit tin gleamed in the thin moonlight as they threw it to and fro like a rugby ball.

But it wasn't rugby they were playing, it was the Game of Crime, and the score was:

LAMONIC BIBBER ROBBERS: ONE BILLION

HEROES UNITED: NIL

Oh, what a terrible, terrible night! The robbers dashed and their teeth gnashed and the rain lashed and the thunder crashed and the lightning flashed and the puddles splashed and the pigs in the fields went oinkety-oink. Yes, the pigs went oinkety-oink.

And as they raced along, Billy William started up with a song and Mr Gum joined in and if you'd been out on the fields that night the blood would have frozen in your veins to hear it. And even just reading it on this page you might feel a little bit chilly for it was the famous and utterly terrifying 'Robbers' Song':

THE ROBBERS' SONG

When the wind is high an' the moon is low
An' the earth is full of dead men's bones
Here we come, creepin' in darkness
Creepin', creepin' along!

When rats an' foxes are prowlin' around
An' the night closes in like a demon's claw
Here we come, into your house
Creepin', creepin' along!

CHORUS:
Wiggle wiggle wiggle!
A-wiggly woo
Bing bong tiddle!
And a yoo-hoo-hoo!
Turn around
And touch your toes
Rob-rob-robbing tonight!

When despair comes knockin'
an' there ain't no hope
An' the ghosts of the past
are rattlin' their chains
Here we come, with our hobnail boots
Creepin', creepin' along!

CHORUS:
Ricky ticky tick
A-Ricky ticky tack
Jingle dingle pingle
Well, fancy that!
Bing bong tiddle
And a yoo-hoo-hoo!
We're rob-rob-robbing tonight, YEAH!

'Right,' said Mr Gum when the song was done. The lightning lit up his face horribly, so you would have sworn he was the Devil himself. Or maybe the Devil's equally bad brother, Jeffrey.

'It'll be light soon an' everyone'll spot us an' catch us into prison,' continued Mr Gum. 'We gotta get off to France.'

'Don't worry 'bout that, me old billionaire,' replied Billy William, getting out his mobile phone. 'I'm calling Monsieur Bellybutton right now.'

ALLO—

'Ah, yes,' smiled Mr Gum. 'Bellybutton. The smelliest man alive.'

Many miles away, a dirty, dirty hand picked up the phone and a horrible stench wafted into the Lamonic Bibber night, faint but unmistakeably disgusting. For you see, Monsieur Bellybutton was so niffy that you could actually smell him all the way down the line from Paris. After a muttered conversation in bad French, Billy put down the phone. Then he threw it at a horse for a laugh.

'It's all arranged,' he told Mr Gum. 'We gotta wait down in Smuggler's Cove for Bellybutton to row over from Paris. Then we jump in his boat an' row back to France. Then we change our names, learn French an' live like powerful kings.'

'I'm gonna change me name to Monsieur le King de la Powerful de la Gum-Gum,' said Mr Gum as they clomped off for Smuggler's Cove.

'An' I'm gonna be Monsieur le King Fantastique de la Butcher de la Billy de la French Toast de la Powerful,' said Billy William.

'An' I'm gonna buy the Eiffel Tower,' laughed

Mr Gum. 'And then I'm gonna smash it to bits an' put up a massive statue of a cockroach.'

By now the sun was coming up, shining miserably through the grey clouds and casting a thin grey light over everything as if there was no joy left in the world and all the footballs had been punctured. Tendrils of mist swirled around the robbers' legs as they came to a windswept cliff top. It was Hangman's Leap and, lordy, it was a wretched place. The cliff face was steep and rocky, and some of the rocks looked a bit like the faces of murderers. Others looked like the faces of thieves or plumbers. Seagulls flew overhead but not nice ones like in paintings. Hangman's Leap attracted only the most dismal seabirds, with one eye and scraggy old feathers and bits of string hanging off their manky legs.

Huffing and puffing, the robbers began the long and treacherous climb down the cliff. It took ages, and Billy William slipped on an empty crisp packet and nearly went a-tumblin' – but somehow they made it to the bottom. Picking their way over the sharp black rocks they were soon at Smuggler's Cove and in they crept, like bad dreams into a postman's head.

It was cold and damp inside the cave. A crab wept with loneliness on the stony floor and a monstrous eel pushed its head out of a hole in the wall and went 'UNNNNGGGH!' An albatross squawked mournfully in the gloom and wolves and vultures sat on the – OK, there weren't any wolves and vultures but it still wasn't very nice. It was a cursed place was Smuggler's Cove, miserable and lonesome and isolated from all civilisation. It was so isolated that there was only a black and white TV. Billy William turned it on.

'Good,' said Mr Gum with satisfaction. 'It's "**Legmash**".'

'**Legmash**' was Mr Gum's new favourite programme. It showed people breaking their legs in real accidents so it was just his type of thing. Billy William started a fire by lighting his own farts and together the robbers settled down to await the arrival of Monsieur Bellybutton.

☐ ☐ ☐

It had been a long night and presently they began to doze off.

'Just think,' yawned Mr Gum. 'This time tomorrow we'll be kinging it up in France an' smashin' things in!'

'Yeah,' yawned Billy William. 'An' throwin' entrails all over Paris an'...'

'Billy,' said Mr Gum sleepily, 'make sure that lid's put down tight on that tin, me old flip-flop. We don't want none of that money escapin'.'

'You do it,' yawned Billy William. 'I'm getting some kip.'

The biscuit tin lay at the cave entrance, its lid half on and half off. After a while a banknote got caught up on the wind and went flying out from the cave, but the robbers didn't notice. They were sound asleep, dreaming of mucking up France.

Chapter 6

Alan Taylor Stays in Bed

The next morning Polly and Friday met in the town square under the historic statue of Some Old Bloke From Ages Ago On A Horse. With heavy hearts, they set off for Boaster's Hill.

'Oh, Friday,' sighed Polly. 'I does hopes Alan Taylor's all right after last night's shenanigans.'

Soon after Polly said this, she and Friday came to the bottom of Boaster's Hill and then a few minutes later they were halfway up and then a bit later after that they were at the top. And it was all thanks to the miracles of legs and walking up hills. As they approached the mansion, they saw the last of the servants making off with a valuable golden peanut. Yes, Alan Taylor's own servants had taken everything and now the mansion was just a great big empty pile of house looking out over the town like a giant's air freshener.

'Servants, you are the worst!' shouted Polly down the hill, her face red with fury and her elbows turquoise with annoyance. 'You oughts to be ashamed, you naughtys! Why, I gots half a mind to write to the Houses of Peppermint an' tell the Prime Minter what's a-goin' on!'

Friday let her rant and rage for he had once

been a young girl himself and he knew what it was like to care about the world with such passions. Eventually Polly was all ranted out and she collapsed in a shrubbery.

'Come hither, little miss,' said Friday sympathetically, helping her out from a geranium. 'For it is now more than ever that Alan Taylor needs us, his true friends. THE TRUTH IS A LEMON MERINGUE!'

So into the mansion they went to find the

unlucky biscuit. The rooms were bare and lonely, the floorboards dusty and creaky beneath the heroes' heels. The wind whistled through the open windows and the majestic kitchen had been completely overrun by a woodlouse. Polly and Friday moved through the rooms calling Alan Taylor's name but there was no answer.

'We checked everywhere,' said Polly worriedly. 'Where IS he?'

Just then they heard a tiny sobbing sound coming from upstairs.

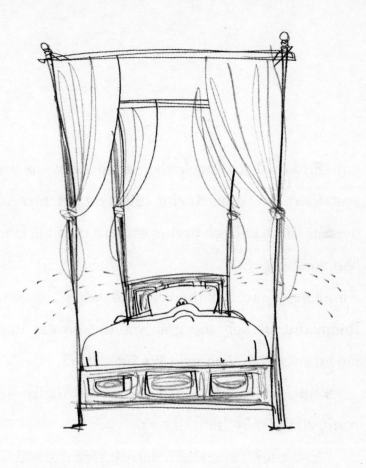

With their heroic ears, they followed the sound
to an enormous four-poster bed in the master
bedroom.

Friday threw back the white satin covers and there lay Alan Taylor, the very picture of despair. He had been crying so hard that his face had gone soggy.

'Leave me be!' he shouted when he saw them and fiercely he grabbed the covers and pulled them back up over his little head.

'But we're your friends,' said Polly in confusion. 'We're here to help you.'

'Friends?' squealed Alan Taylor. 'That's a

laugh! You're just like all the others. You only like me when I've got money! The rest of the time you laugh behind my back. And you call me names like "Cake Face Alan" and "Crumb Boy", just like they did at school!'

'But we don't likes you for your money,' pleaded Polly. 'We likes you for who you really are.'

'Yeah, right,' snorted Alan Taylor. 'Just like the servants. Oh, they were friendly enough when I was rich. They laughed at my jokes and tickled me for my amusement. But all the time they were just after my cash, my antiques and my valuable golden peanut.'

'But we're not like them, can't you see?' protested Polly. 'Plus we're gonna catch the robbers into prison an' gets back all your money for you!'

'Yeah, and once I'm rich again you'll pretend to be my friends again, I suppose,' replied the unhappy biscuit. 'Well, I'm not having it. I'm sick and tired of being made fun of and I'm going to stay in bed FOREVER. I don't need any so-called "friends". I don't need anybody!'

'But Alan Taylo—'

'GET OUT!' he squealed. 'I never want to see either of you again!'

'Come on, little miss,' said Friday solemnly. 'Let's leave him be.'

And he took Polly's hand and led her

towards the door. But at the last moment Polly ran back to the bed, hot tears rolling down her pretty face.

'Alan Taylor, I d-dunno what's got into you,' sobbed Polly. 'But I knows you d-don't mean it. An' I b-brought you a present, only you was so angry I nearly forgot 'bout it.'

She reached into her skirt pocket and pulled out a fifty pence piece.

'There,' she said, pressing the coin into his

weeny brown hand. 'It's everythin' what I got in my piggy bank. I was savin' it towards a computer but I w-wants you to have it, just in case we can't finds your riches.'

Alan Taylor just stared at the coin. He didn't even say 'thank you'. It was more than Polly could bear. With one final sob she turned and fled from the room, her face buried in her hands.

Friday stood there for a moment longer, gazing down at the ungrateful biscuit in his enormous white bed. 'The truth is a lemon meringue,' said Friday very quietly and he shook his head. 'That's all I've got to say to you, my friend.'

Chapter 7
On the Trail of the Money

Friday twirled his imaginary detective's moustache wearily.

'I admit it,' he said as he and Polly sat eating lunch in the *Chapter 7 Café*. 'This case is too tough even for me.'

They had been searching all morning but they hadn't found any robbers, not even one.

'Oh, Friday,' said Polly, looking despondently at her jacket potato. It wasn't the jacket potato's fault, she just felt despondent anyway.

'Oh, Polly,' said Friday, looking despondently at his jacket potato because he wished he'd ordered the pasta instead. And together they sat there, looking despondently at jacket potatoes.

But suddenly Polly sat bolt upright.

'Hey!' she exclaimed. 'What's that a-flutterin' outside the window?'

'It's just a twenty pound note,' said Friday despondently. 'I wish I'd ordered the pasta.'

'But don't you gets it?' explained Polly. 'It must be the trail of the robbers at last!'

'Hot wigwams, you're right!' shouted Friday. 'To the Alancopter! I mean, to the motorbike!'

And leaving their lunches untouched, they ran outside.

At the next table Jonathan Ripples and Martin Launderette watched them go.

'I wonder what that's all about,' said Jonathan Ripples.

'Never mind that,' said Martin eagerly. 'Try your pea soup.'

'Urgh!' said Jonathan R., swallowing down a spoonful. 'Someone's put torn-up pieces of newspaper in it!'

'Who'd do a thing like that?' said Martin Launderette innocently, taking out his red notebook.

Another victory, he wrote. The pea soup joke was HILARIOUS.

Friday's motorbike was parked outside on the high street.

'Hop on, Polly!' he shouted, starting the bike up with a roar.

'Don't roar like that,' said Polly. 'It scares me.'

'Sorry,' said Friday and stopped roaring. He

revved the engine and off they zoomed. Before too long they came across another banknote blowing on the wind. Soon after that they saw one stuck in a hedge and soon after that they saw one stuck in a pop star's haircut.

'We's on the right track!' cried Polly. On, on they went, and all the while they saw money. Money, money, money, flapping on the wind or stuck in bushes or being eaten by magpies and tramps.

Soon they had left the town far behind and Polly began to get a little worried. They were riding through strange fields with twisted up trees and scarecrows with no heads. Sinister sounds like 'YIM!', 'KOOBLES!' and 'BEEF!' rang out from the undergrowth and who knew what creatures lurked therein? Storm clouds were gathering and the day had grown dark and threatening.

'Where is we, Frides?' Polly whispered.

'I'm not sure, little miss,' replied Friday.

'But have faith. The Universe is a mysterious place, and everything happens for a reason. Except for stinging nettles. They're just a nuisance. But not to worry, there's none 'round here!'

Now, Friday had barely said these knowledgeable words when the motorbike broke down in the middle of a great big patch of stinging nettles. Huge ones they were, towering higher than Polly's head and full of bad pains for anyone who tried to mess with them.

'Brummigans!' exclaimed Friday. 'We'll have to walk from here.'

'Look at all them nettlers,' trembled Polly. 'Just a-waitin' to sting us to bits though we done nothin' to them!'

'Fear not, little miss,' said Friday, heaving her on to his shoulders. 'Though I am old, my legs are as strong as – OUCH! OOH! OW!'

'You brave, brave man,' said Polly from her position of safety above the treacherous plants. It was a bit unlucky that Friday had chosen to wear shorts that day and no shoes or socks, but there you go. That's life.

109

'OUCH! OOH! BLIMEY! FLAN! EEK! MOOO! FLURTLE!' grimaced Friday as he picked his way through the nettles. They seemed to go on forever but he kept at it, because he was a force for good and his heart was true and his feet were bare. At last they reached the edge of the field and there Friday collapsed like a broken gypsy in the scrubby grass.

'Go on without me,' he gasped, his legs covered in painful white blisters. 'I'll ... be ... all right ...'

'I won't leaves you, Friday!' said Polly, cradling his head in her arms. 'I'll stay with you forev–'

Just then they heard a voice coming from somewhere below.

'Oi! Caterpillar Joe! I can't wait to escape to France with all that money what we stole,' someone cackled.

'It's the robbers!' whispered Friday urgently. 'Now go, Polly. Go and save the day with your Pollyness!'

Chapter 8

Smuggler's Cove

With one last glance back at Friday, Polly pushed through the long tall grass and found herself on a windswept cliff top. It was Hangman's Leap and, lordy, it was a more wretched place than ever.

Remember those rocks that looked a bit like nasty faces? Well, they were still there. In fact, there were even more of them than before, don't ask me how, but there were. And those manky seagulls with one eye and stuff? There were more of them too, because they'd been up all night breeding new and even more disgusting ones. Some of the new seagulls smoked cigarettes and had tattoos on their wings.

Altogether it was a frightful scene, made even worse by the rain and the dark thundery skies above but Polly had work to do. She peered over the cliff edge and could just make out two tiny figures on the beach below, striking evil poses.

'Those flippin' roo-de-lallies!' she muttered and without further thought she started down the cliff.

Down on the rocks Mr Gum was looking out to sea with a powerful telescope he'd made from a jar of mustard, a rolled-up magazine and a powerful telescope.

'There he is!' he shouted gleefully as a small wooden fishing boat appeared on the horizon. 'It's Monsieur Bellybutton!'

'Are you sure?' asked Billy William, but at that moment the wind changed direction and the most horrendous stench came to their noses. It smelt like a zoo had married a gigantic fart. Only it was even worse than that.

'Oh, yes,' said Mr Gum, his eyebrows curling up and turning crispy with the pong. 'It's him all right!'

'Bonjour Monsieur Gum, bonjour Monsieur Billy!' shouted Bellybutton as he rowed into Smuggler's Cove.

You know in cartoons when they do wavy lines to show that something smells bad? Like there'll be a rotten fish head or something and they'll do wavy lines coming off of it? Well, I'm not lying but Monsieur Bellybutton actually had those wavy lines coming off of him IN REAL LIFE. He had never once taken a bath and he was quite an old man so just think about it.

'Bonjour,' the two villains cried in pleasure. You see, incredible as it was, they actually *liked* the smell of Monsieur Bellybutton.

'Mmm,' said Mr Gum, inhaling long and hard. 'He's smellin' even riper than last year. Lovely!'

Polly was nearly at the bottom of the cliff when the smell of Bellybutton hit her like invisible boxing gloves filled with gorgonzola. She fell to her knees, clutching her nose in agony, but even so the smell found a way in, bringing tears to her eyes and clouding her thoughts.

'I dunno what that's about,' said Polly through gritted teeth. 'But them robbers needs sortin' out!'

Determinedly she stuffed a bunch of daisies up her nostrils and continued on. The further down she climbed, the stronger the smell became. The daisies shrivelled up and went brown. Seagulls fell out of the sky, landing with thumps all around her, but still she did not falter. And that's what Pollyness is all about.

Finally she reached the bottom of the cliff. The wind changed direction once more and she could breathe again, which is very helpful for living.

And now she saw where the stink was coming from. A smellster Frenchman with wavy lines coming off of him IN REAL LIFE was helping Mr Gum into a mucky fishing boat encrusted with barnacles. Billy William was already on board, the biscuit tin clutched to his scrawny chest.

'Hey! Robbers!' shouted Polly. 'I'm arrestin' you in the name of the Laws!'

'You!' spat Mr Gum, spinning round in fury. 'How'd you find us, you meddler? We never left no tracks to follow!'

But even as he spoke, a tenner flew into the air and Mr Gum knew the truth of Billy William's laziness at putting lids on biscuit tins properly.

'You MUNCHER!' shouted Mr Gum,

slapping the careless butcher round the chops. 'I
TOLD you to sort out that lid!'

'Robbers, your games is up,' said Polly

sternly. 'An' don't you think you can float off to France and muck everything up over there too. I'm not havin' it!'

'Oh, yeah?' sneered Mr Gum. 'What you gonna do? You're just a stupid little girl an' you can't do nothin' against powerful kings like me an' Billy.'

Like lightning Mr Gum reached down and grabbed a heavy fishing net dripping with slime and dead lobsters. Running up the beach, he chucked it at Polly and before she knew what was happening she was down on the sands, buried under its filthy weight. Struggling against it was no good. It was just one of those nets you can't beat with struggling.

'Au revoir!' shouted Mr Gum as Monsieur Bellybutton started to row away.

'Au revoir,' replied Polly politely. 'I mean – Hey! Come back here, you crimers!'

But the boat was soon just a tiny speck on the horizon and the day was lost.

❧ ❧ ❧

How long Polly lay under that net she didn't know. Was it minutes? Hours? Years? Probably not years. Anyway, there she lay – helpless and crying with rage.

'Friday could be dead up on that cliff an' them robbers has escaped an' I hates it!' she sobbed. 'It ain't fair an' the world's rubbish an' I don't care 'bout nothin' no more so shut up!'

Eventually she had no more tears left to shed. She lay there, exhausted, and her eyes they did close, and soon she was dreaming the strangest dream . . .

Alan Taylor was there and he was nibbling away at the net with his little sharp teeth, nibbling, nibbling, nibbling.

A dead lobster fell on his head but he just pushed it off and went on nibbling. Polly could hear his electric muscles whirring away and she could see his kind brave face full of concentration and raisins...

Nibble, nibble, nibble. Whirr, whirr, whirr.

Nibble, nibble, nibble. Whirr, whirr, whirr.

Nibble! Whirr!

Nibble! Whirr!

Nibble, nibble, nibble. Whirr, whirr, whirr...

Polly opened one eye and there was the Biscuit Billionaire himself. It wasn't no dream after all! He was standing proudly on the sands with bits of net in his teeth, his doughy body protected from the rain by a miniature Superman cape which made him look like Batman.

'A.T.!' gasped Polly, climbing out of the net. 'Is it really you?'

'It's me, all right,' said he. 'I've come to my senses and got out of bed. And now to catch those robbers!'

'But how we gonna gets 'em?' asked Polly. 'For we haven't no boat an' we can't just swim out there, you insaner!'

'No,' said Alan Taylor. 'But I know someone who can.'

He gave a high-pitched whistle and suddenly a face Polly knew well appeared from behind a rock. Not just a face on its own though, that would be horrible. It was attached to a body Polly knew well too.

'I can't believes it!' she cried, running up to hug her fat golden friend. For it was Jake, that massive whopper of a dog, come to the rescue at last.

Chapter 9
Hooray for Friendship!

Jake gave a happy bark and slobbered all over Polly with joy and together they had a bit of a romp on the rocks, with tickling and rolling around and woofing and suchlike.

'You know each other?' asked Alan Taylor.

'Are you kidding?' said Polly. 'Me an' Jake,

we're friends of old!'

'How extraordinary,' said Alan Taylor. 'He followed me all the way here, almost as if he wanted to help.'

'Yeah,' said Polly, stroking Jake's tongue. 'Cos he's the cleverest hero dog ever, an' he knew we was in troubles!'

Actually, Jake had just been wandering along looking for insects to eat but never mind. The important thing was that he was there.

Alan Taylor hopped on to his great broad head and Polly hopped on to his massive whopper back.

'Rinky-dink-dink!' she cried, and with that the magnificent canine flopped into the sea and started up his Doggy Paddler 2000s, otherwise

known as his legs. Alan Taylor tugged at Jake's ears to steer him, and Polly was in charge of fuel, which meant cramming dog biscuits into his mouth. (She'd been carrying around dozens of them in her skirt pocket all summer, in case Jake showed up. To be honest, it was a relief to finally get rid of them.)

Meanwhile, back on the boat the robbers were just lazing around doing nothing much. They weren't even rowing, they were just letting the boat drift off to France of its own accord. Billy William was impressing Monsieur Bellybutton by eating a fifty pound note and Mr Gum was looking for dolphins to scowl at.

'Aha!' he said, spying a great big one on the starboard side. 'Now for some quality scowlin'!'

But as it came closer Mr Gum saw that it wasn't a dolphin after all. It was Jake, carrying his cargo of heroes.

And the next moment the glorious beast erupted from the waters like a furry referee and landed in the boat with an enormous wet crash. His whopper paws went scrabbling about all over the place and got Billy William right in the never-you-minds.

'Ooof,' yipped Billy, and that was him out of the action.

'MEDDLERS!' screamed Mr Gum, grabbing the biscuit tin and reaching for a bashing stick, but Alan Taylor jumped at him in a heroic frenzy, his Superman cape streaming out behind him. He landed on the biscuit tin and sunk his teeth into Mr Gum's right hand.

'Shabba me whiskers!' wailed Mr Gum. 'That hurts like a rascal!' He waved his hand about, trying to dislodge Alan Taylor, but when it came down to it he was just a lame-o coward and he had to let go.

'Whimper!' he remarked, retreating to the

end of the boat. But there was no place to run and he couldn't swim, and why? Because he couldn't be bothered.

Working fast, Polly and Alan Taylor tied up Mr Gum and Billy William. Then Polly turned to their evil-smelling accomplice.

'You a bad one, all right,' she said, looking Monsieur Bellybutton up and down. 'But maybe there's hopes for you yet. Get in this thing,' she commanded, pointing to a medieval catapult that stood in one corner of the boat.

Monsieur Bellybutton took one look at Jake's big teeth and climbed inside, sobbing in terror.

'Stand back!' said Polly and –

SSPLLLANNNNG!

Monsieur Bellybutton shot out of the catapult and over the waves.

'NNNNNNNNNNNNNNNNNNNNNNNNON!' he screamed in slow-motion, which is the French for 'NNNNNNNNNNNNNNNNNNNNNNNNNO!'

Because for the first time in his grubulent life, Monsieur Bellybutton was about to have a bath.

LE SPLASH!

In he went. The sea began to boil up all around him as layer after layer of dirt finally met its arch enemy – water. Monsieur Bellybutton coughed and choked and hiccuped but to no avail.

The dirt was losing and at long last, after all those years, the world was free of his atrocious fragrance. A vast wave full of laughing starfish and seahorses swept him up and carried him all the way back to Paris, and never did he hassle anybody again but instead he became the loveliest grandfather you could imagine, and he knew stories and songs about happy happy mice.

♙ ♙ ♙

But never mind that now, because Polly and Alan Taylor were rowing back to land with the defeated robbers mumbling and moaning at their feet. As they approached the shore they saw an excited figure hobbling over the rocks and shouting:

'THE TRUTH IS A LEMON MERINGUE!

THE TRUTH IS A LEMON MERINGUE! THE TRUTH IS A LEMON MERINGUE! THE TRUTH IS A LEMON MERINGUE! THE TRUTH IS A LEMON MERINGUE!'

'Do you think that's Friday?' asked Alan Taylor.

'I wouldn't be surprised,' said Polly, who knew her friend well.

And indeed it was he. As soon as the boat reached land, the heroes all ran up to give him '*friendship* medals', which means hugs.

'Careful!' cautioned Friday as they hugged away. 'I'm still in pain.'

And seeing Friday's brave legs all covered in blisters, Polly suddenly fell silent to remember what he'd been through – stinging nettles. Big ones.

And so the heroes made their way back up Hangman's Leap with Mr Gum and Billy William tied firmly to Jake's furry back. When finally they reached the top of the cliff Alan Taylor cleared his throat to make a speech and also to get rid of a whelk that had got in there.

'Polly,' he began, 'if it weren't for you I never would have discovered the true meaning of *friendship*.'

'Eh?' said Polly in surprise.

'It's true,' said Alan Taylor, holding up a small shiny object for all to see. 'For you gave me this fifty pence piece, though it was all the money you had in the world. And as I lay in bed feeling sorry for myself I realised it is *friendship* that is important in life, not money.'

He handed Polly back her coin and then continued.

'Now,' he speeched. 'Time to do something I should have done a long time ago. This –' he said, holding up the biscuit tin, 'this has brought me only misery and it's stopped me from seeing what true friends are, and things like that.'

And before anyone could stop him he took the lid off the tin and flung its contents into the wind. Everyone watched in awe as the money tumbled out and went flying over the ocean like expensive seagulls.

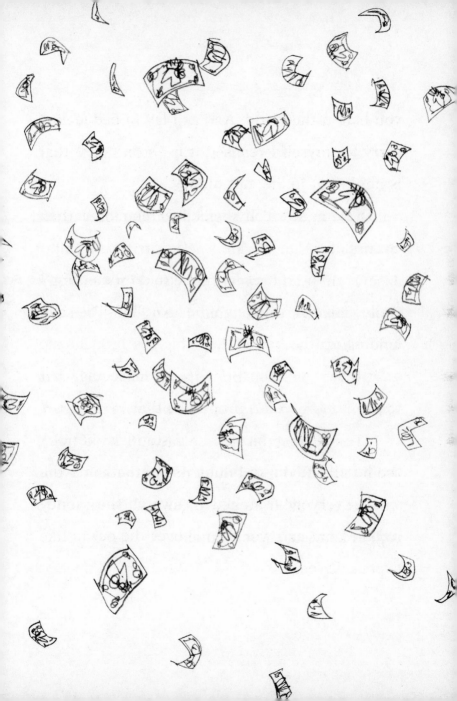

All those millions. It seemed to take forever but eventually Alan Taylor was left with an empty biscuit tin – and something else. For a moment Polly couldn't think what it was but then she understood.

Why, she thought, *I never once seen him smilin' before! Not a proper smile from the heart.*

For a great burden seemed to have fallen from Alan Taylor's shoulders. As the sun came out, he grinned from ear to ear and he looked to Polly like the richest man alive.

Chapter 10
The Spirit of the Rainbow

All of a sudden Mr Gum and Billy William started straining at their ropes and trying to escape, their faces pale with fright.

'It's h-him,' stuttered Mr Gum, pointing to a great haystack he could have sworn hadn't been there a moment earlier. A little boy was climbing out of it, laughing with delight, and as he approached the last of the clouds seemed to disappear from the sky.

And now, a lovely warm feeling came over Polly as if someone were baking lasagne in her veins. She felt that all the wrongs of the world would be righted and all the rights of the world would carry on being right and perhaps become even more right somehow. She looked at Alan

Taylor and Friday and saw they felt it too.

'Spirit of the Rainbow!' laughed Polly, clapping her hands. 'Can it really be you?'

'Yes, child,' he said, though he was no older than she. 'You and your friends have done well and learned lessons. Once more the world is glowing with happy colours.'

'Sir, we have never met before,' said Alan Taylor with a respectful bow. 'Yet you seem familiar, as if I have seen you in brief moments of happiness.'

'It may be so,' replied the Spirit of the Rainbow with his honest mouth. 'For whenever a baby dribbles with joy, I am there. Whenever a cat jumps into a cardboard box and makes everyone laugh, I am there. Whenever someone blows a bubble and it rises on the wind and doesn't pop for ages, I am there. And now, old man,' he said, turning to Friday, 'look around this cliff top for I believe there are plants of healing to be found which will ease your wounded legs.'

Looking around Friday saw a clump of enormous green dock leaves which he could have sworn hadn't been there a moment earlier. He rubbed them on his legs and instantly the angry white blisters were gone and his legs were better than ever and not so hairy.

Then the Spirit of the Rainbow turned to address the robbers.

'Robbers,' he began earnestly, 'when will you realise that the world is a place of harmony and getting along with people? For your greed has undone you and now –'

'Spirit!' called a voice from over the hills. 'Come on or we'll be late!'

'Oops,' said the Spirit of the Rainbow, looking at his watch. 'I've gotta go or my Mum'll kill me. We're visting my Aunt.'

And he chucked them a handful of fruit chews and off he ran.

It was a long walk back to Lamonic Bibber but it was a happy one. Friday got out his favourite flute and played a march called 'The Captain of the

Ants' and Alan Taylor surprised everyone by pointing out features of the landscape and teaching them about the natural world as they went.

'See that?' he said, pointing to a rock. 'That is a rock. And those colourful things over there? They are known as flowers.'

'Why, you're a changed man,' said Friday in wonder.

'Yes, I love learning and education,' said Alan Taylor. 'All that money made me forget how

much I REALLY have to offer the world.'

But here's the thing. In all the fun and learning Mr Gum and Billy William were forgotten and they managed to escape by sawing through the ropes with their sharp fingernails.

'Let's get out of here, Caterpillar Joe,' whispered Mr Gum and off they tiptoed in their hobnail boots. And where they went nobody knows but the wind.

Chapter 11
The Festival of the Leaves

*I*t was nearly sunset when the heroes finally reached Lamonic Bibber once more.

'Look,' said Polly happily. All the good people of the town were out on the streets, rejoicing and waving flags and playing kiss chase.

And the town square was full of long wooden benches laden with food.

'There seems to be a feast going on,' said Alan Taylor.

'Not just any feast,' remarked Friday. 'Today must be the first day of autumn. It's the Festival of the Leaves!'

'Oh, I forgot all about the Festival of the Leaves!' said Polly. 'I loves it so!'

'It's true,' announced the warm voice of David Casserole, the town mayor. 'Look, the first leaf fell today. Who shall be this year's King of Autumn?' he challenged, holding up the little golden leaf.

'The Biscuit Billionaire!' responded the crowd. 'The Biscuit Billionaire! Now that he's got his money back we can have funfairs again!'

'No,' said Alan Taylor, climbing on to Friday's head for more speech action. 'I'm no longer a rich man,' he told the crowd. 'But if you can find it in your hearts to love me for who I am, I will turn my mansion into a school called 𝕾𝖆𝖎𝖓𝖙 𝕻𝖙𝖊𝖗𝖔𝖉𝖆𝖈𝖙𝖞𝖑'𝖘 𝕾𝖈𝖍𝖔𝖔𝖑 𝕱𝖔𝖗 𝕿𝖍𝖊 𝕻𝖔𝖔𝖗 and I will teach all the poor children and orphans about education and learning. And no one will tease anyone there or call each other bad names,' he added firmly.

'Fair enough!' shouted the crowd.

'You are truly our King of Autumn!' boomed David Casserole, pinning the leaf on to Alan Taylor's chest whilst pretty ladies crowned him with acorns and conkers. And Alan Taylor grinned happily as he led the townsfolk in a merry jig, for finally he had been accepted.

Well, there wasn't much to say after all that. It was a time for feasts and rejoicing. Friday played the piano that stood in the town square and Old Granny fell over from too much sherry and everyone saw the weird veins in her old legs, and

Jonathan Ripples found a red notebook a-lying on the ground. He turned to the front page and read:

That fatty Ripples thinks he's so clever but I'll have the last laugh!

'Hmm,' he frowned, chewing on a roast ox leg, 'I recognise this handwriting.'

He found Martin Launderette cowering behind a lamp post and took him to one side.

'Martin,' he said, holding up the notebook, 'this isn't very nice.'

'I know,' said Martin Launderette, with a sigh. 'I'm ashamed of myself.'

'I'm afraid I'm going to have to sit on you now to teach you a lesson,' said Jonathan Ripples sadly. 'This is going to hurt me more than it will hurt you.'

But how wrong can you be? It didn't hurt Jonathan Ripples one bit.

By midnight the partying and feasting was dying down and the stars hung friendly in the sky. Polly sat with her companions in the shadowy square, tired but happy. Jake was licking up spilt ox gravy, Alan Taylor lay contentedly in a heap of leaves and Friday was strumming quietly on a blue guitar.

As he strummed, someone appeared at the far end of the town square. It was Mrs Lovely, who ran the sweet shop, and not only that, she was Friday's wife too.

'Mrs Lovely!' cried Friday, and dropping his guitar he swept her up in his lovey dovey arms and everyone went 'aaaaaaaah'.

'Mrs Lovely, where you been all this time?' asked Polly.

'Away in the mountains, gathering secret herbs for my sweets,' she trilled. 'Did I miss anything?'

And a shooting star shot by like a cornflake falling out of God's breakfast, and the Man in the Moon tried to eat it but he missed. And the heroic friends sat in the old town square wondering what adventures they'd have next and Friday stuck a breadstick up his nose to impress everyone and it broke off and the crumbs went down his throat and made him cough a bit.

And then, just when he thought he couldn't possibly be any happier, Alan Taylor gasped in astonishment. *For I am no longer made of gingerbread!* he thought. *At last I am a real man!*

Then he took a closer look at himself and realised he had made a mistake. 'Oh,' he sighed. 'I'm still a gingerbread man with electric muscles after all. Well, never mind. Everything else worked out OK.'

THE END

HELLO.

Here's what. You might think you know everything there is to know about Lamonic Bibber and the townsfolk who live there. But do you really? Do you? DO YOU?

No! No! NO! You do not. So stop showing off.

You see, there is always more to learn about those crazy old townsfolk and that is why we proudly present . . .

THE LAMONIC LISTS

Polly's Favourite Ever Books, shut up cos it's true

1 'The Shark Who Lived On The Moon' by Greg Kingsley

2 'Cobbler Wins The Prizes' by Mimsy Rogers

3 'Help, I'm A Moron' by Timothy Face

4 'Come Back, Burpy Jenkins!' by Samantha Brown

5 'My Life As A Tangerine' by Eric P. Madman

6 'Dinkles, The World's Fattest Parrot' by Reg Webb

7 'The Mystery Of The Mysterious Mystery'
   by Janet Zigzag

8 'Cobbler Meets The Poo Rabbits' by Mimsy Rogers

9 'Herzog' by Saul Bellow

10 'You Can Do It, Cobbler!' by Mimsy Rogers

10 Things Friday O'Leary Is Secretly a Bit Scared of

1 Big dogs

2 Moths

3 Big dog with a moth stuck in its fur

4 Those things over there in the corner

5 'Cobbler Meets The Poo Rabbits' by Mimsy Rogers

6 Calendars

7 Being eaten alive by antelopes

8 Not being eaten alive by antelopes*

9 The number 9

10 Going to sleep and when you wake up you're in Argentina and everyone's laughing at you in a foreign language*

*This actually happened to Friday once

10 Words Billy William the Third Pronounces Funny

WORD	HOW BWIII SAYS IT
1 Funny	Funty
2 England	Engerland
3 Hospital	Hoppital
4 Dinosaur	Minotaur
5 Minotaur	Rhino war
6 Mystery	Mittersy
7 Dentist	Dennist
8 Pumpkin	Plumpkin
9 Screwdriver	Matthew Robinson
10 Fountain	(Not sure because no one's ever heard him say it. It's a mittersy.)

Mr Gum's Top T.V Programmes of All Time

1 'BAG OF STICKS'
(A picture of a bag of sticks for half an hour)

2 'BAG OF STICKS CHRISTMAS SPECIAL'
(A dead robin lying by the bag of sticks)

3 'LEGMASH'
(People breaking their legs in real accidents)

4 'NO! PUT THAT DOWN!'
(Parents in supermarkets refusing to buy their children sweets)

5 'BAG OF STICKS: BEHIND THE MAGIC'
(4-hour-documentary about the making of 'Bag of Sticks', including interviews with the director, the cameraman and the dead robin)

Mrs Lovely's Top 5 Sweet Ingredients

1 Sorry, can't tell you, it's a secret

2 Another secret

3 Forget it, this one's just too secret to tell

4 Sorry, no

5 Aniseed

Martin Launderette's Favourite Washing Machine Settings

1 COLD WASH

2 COLD WASH, EXTRA SPIN

3 GENTLE RINSE

4 DELICATE WASH, NO SPIN (good for woollens)

5 Just chuck it all in, turn it up as high as it goes and see what happens

Some Little-Known Facts About Old Granny

1 Old Granny was always called Old Granny, even when she was a little girl

2 Old Granny is a bit deaf. I said, OLD GRANNY IS A BIT DEAF!

3 Old Granny once won the Olympics by accident when she ran for a bus

4 Old Granny has got a tattoo of Queen Victoria on her ankle

5 Queen Victoria had a tattoo of Old Granny on her ankle

6 Old Granny holds the world record for being Old Granny

7 Old Granny can't whistle no good. It's all out of tune

8 Old Granny can fly

9 Not really

10 Old Granny can't speak Russian

10 of the Most Expensive Things
in Alan Taylor's Mansion

1 Portrait of Leonardo da Vinci painted by Mona Lisa

2 Shakespeare's right hand in a jar

3 Piece of paper with first ever game of noughts
   and crosses on it*

4 A really nice table

5 Machine that can video your dreams

6 A cat with ten thousand pounds tied on to its tail

7 Suit of armour worn by Beethoven in a fight
   against Mozart

8 Largest banana ever grown (nearly twice the size
   of normal banana)

9 Valuable golden peanut

10 Signed photo of the Loch Ness Monster

*It was a draw

About the Illustrator

David Tazzyman lives in South London with his girlfriend, Melanie, and their three children. He grew up in Leicester, studied illustration at Manchester Metropolitan University and then travelled around Asia for three years before moving to London in 1997. He likes football, cricket, biscuits, music and drawing. He dislikes celery.

About the Author

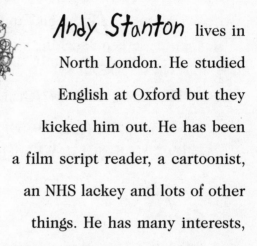

Andy Stanton lives in North London. He studied English at Oxford but they kicked him out. He has been a film script reader, a cartoonist, an NHS lackey and lots of other things. He has many interests, but best of all he likes cartoons, books and music (even jazz). One day he'd like to live in New York or Berlin or one of those places because he's got fantasies of bohemia. His favourite expression is 'Please, sir,' and his favourite word is 'proletariat'. This is his second book.

Surf the Net in Style at . . .

MRGUM.CO.UK

Why do exercise and healthy outdoors pursuits when you can sit all hunched up in front of a tiny computer screen, laughing your little face off at the all-bonkers, 82% official

OFFICIAL MR GUM OFFICIAL WEBSITE?!

Yes, no, it's true! The OFFICIAL MR GUM OFFICIAL WEBSITE features:

- *Things!*
- *Games!*
- *Photos* of the author with beard and without!
- *Videos* including an episode of Bag of Sticks
- *Loud noises!*
- *Words* like 'YANKLE', 'BLITTLER' and 'FLOINK'!
- *Crafty Tom* – the Tyrannosaurus rex with a heart of gold!*

You'll never need to go outdoors again!

*Actual website may not include Crafty Tom

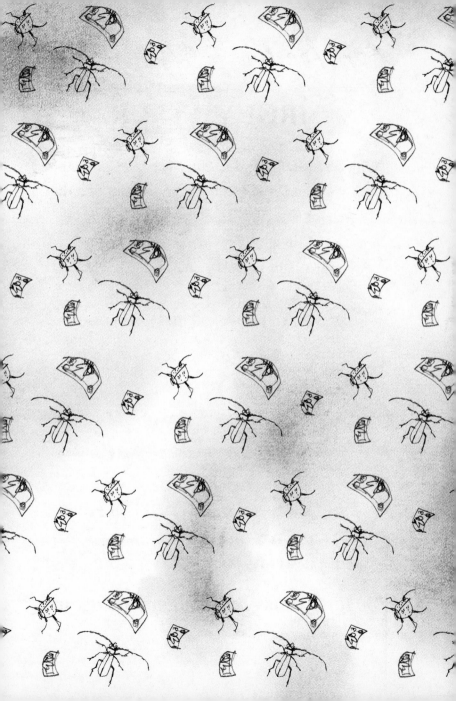

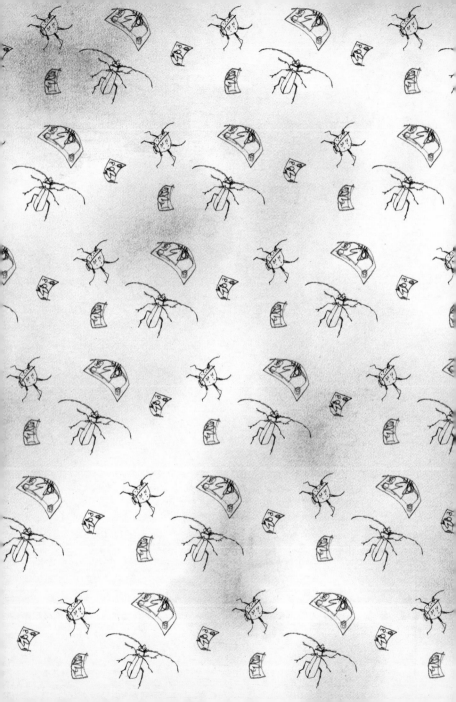